What is this thing called Aloha

Robert James

Published and distributed by
ISLAND HERITAGE PUBLISHING
ISBN 0-89610-404-4

Address orders and correspondence to:

ISLAND HERITAGE
P   U   B   L   I   S   H   I   N   G

94-411 Kō'aki Street
Waipahu, Hawai'i 96797
Telephone 808-564-8800
To order 800-468-2800
www.islandheritage.com

Printed in Hong Kong
First edition, Fourth printing 2005

Photography by
Veronica Carmona

Book design by
Sachi Kuwahara Goodwin

Introduction

It has been said that the word "aloha" actually has two definitions. "Alo" means the center or heart of the universe, while "ha" is the breath or spirit of the Creator.

It has also been said that aloha cannot be found outside of ourselves. It can only be uncovered at the center of our hearts. That is where it lives. That is where it awaits us.

And once found, aloha makes our lives whole, gives power to our words, fills our actions with purpose, and assures that our every thought is of benefit to each other and to the world around us.

Aloha is the essence of the Creator's love, and when that love is expressed through our voices, our minds, our hearts, and our hands, the world becomes a better place.

You might ask, "How can this be? There are millions and millions of hearts in the world, how can aloha be found in mine?"

There is only one heart, one center, one spirit, one aloha. Find aloha at the core of your own being and you will have instantly found it in everyone and everything.

One heart
One center
One spirit
One aloha

Robert James

Preface

There is something exceptional about early mornings in Hawai'i. They bring a sense of tranquillity, promise, and hope that I cannot find at any other time of day. It is for that reason that I meditate before dawn comes, before the "noise" of working, parenting, and living take over my head and heart. During this time, I succumb to the silence.

It was during one of these sessions that one answer to the question, "What is aloha?" presented itself to me.

"Aloha exists beyond motives, desires, or opinions. It is sustained by love, fortified by compassion, and expands in power and beauty as we give it away to all who come into our lives." From somewhere out of the stillness of my inner being, that thought arose and I later wrote it down.

And so it was with all of the writings in this book. They are the results of quiet receptiveness. As someone once said, "When the spirit speaks, the spirit listens." I truly hope that these simple offerings find a welcome home in the hearts, minds, and souls of all who read them.

Robert James

Prologue

At an outdoor wedding, I overheard
a man, a guest who was not from the Islands,
ask the Hawaiian minister who had just
performed the wedding ceremony, "What is
the thing called, 'aloha'?"

The old minister placed both of his hands on
the man's shoulders and replied, "Aloha is the
'life' of Hawai'i."

Much like the scent of a flower,
aloha emanates from the heart.
Those who are centered in aloha
cannot help but shower unending
love and beauty on the world.

The winds sing of it, the rain falls
through it, the palms move to it,
the earth churns with it, the ocean
rolls in it. It is spirit moving form.
It is the soul of all creation.
It is aloha.

Like seeds on the wind, let your aloha find a home in every soul you meet.

Meditating or thinking deeply about aloha is like sitting by a peaceful, rejuvenating river of goodness. If you sit there often enough and long enough a wonderful thing begins to happen. In time, you become such a part of the river of aloha that it effortlessly flows through you and into the world where it is so needed.

The existence of aloha is not an abstraction. Feel it now. It is in your blood. It is in your bones. It is in your mind, heart, and soul. Find it in the silent wonder of yourself.

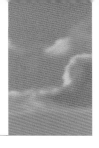

Aloha resides in the quietest room of your heart. Go there daily, sit with it, learn its ways, be still and become one with it. Then bring it out for all the world to share.

It is easy to love those most dear
to you. Aloha makes it possible for
you to love your larger family,
humanity.

Aloha will not tolerate exclusion of any kind. Light is its color. Love is its blood.

A loving wish, a kind gesture, a
thank you. All are acts of aloha.

We have two voices within ourselves. One is in our head, the other is in our heart. One says, "I want!", "I need!", "I must have this!" It is filled with greed, envy, anger, and plotting. Aloha, the other voice, says, "If I have, let me share it with others. If I dream, may it serve the greater good."

Aloha confirms the power of the spirit living in each of us and asks that we bring forth that spirit through our positive actions.

Aloha is found in silence, lived in peace, and passed on in love.

Aloha exists beyond motives,
desires, or opinions. It is sustained
by love, fortified by compassion,
and it expands in power and beauty
as we give it away to all who come
into our lives.

Aloha is not an object,
it is the spirit of right action.

To those who believe in God,
aloha is an expression of God's
love for us all. To those who don't
believe, aloha is an example of our
fundamental goodness.

The more you use your aloha, the stronger it flows through you.

Does aloha love? Yes!

Does aloha judge? Never.

Giving our aloha to others is the only way of keeping it.

Aloha often means performing
right actions in the presence of the
wrong actions of others.

Aloha is balance, patience,
harmony, peace, tolerance, and
boundless love.

Aloha is the epitome of the perfect alchemist. It can change evil into good, cruelty into caring, and hate into love.

A compassionate tear is
aloha made visible.

Do something wonderful for someone and do it completely anonymously. That is an act of aloha.

The light of aloha can never be extinguished. Never! But it can be hidden from you by fear, greed, possessiveness, and cruelty.

Give in to your aloha, trust in it,
follow its urgings, and watch as it
guides your life.

Aloha lives in our hearts and has
the courage of a thousand lions.

Aloha is all good, all wise, all love.

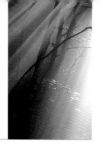

The world needs the light of aloha.
It needs the peace of it, the
blessing of it, and the purifying
qualities it possesses.

The more you are able to let aloha
pour from yourself through your
thoughts, wishes, prayers, and
external actions, the more you
brighten the world.

When your actions are guided by the power of aloha, they enter the beings of others as unity, harmony, peace, and love.

Notes